I could not have brought this book into being without the following people. I will be forever grateful to each one of them.

Laura, Barbie and Liz, for your editorial challenges, some of which I really didnt want to hear, but all of which were valuable.

Margaret for my beautiful cover picture..

All of you who have told me this was worth publishing and that people will want to read it!

Thank you to each of you.

CAUGHT

We were washing the nets after a really rotten night's fishing, feeling pretty hacked off, when there He was. Well, we actually saw the crowd of people first and wondered what was going on as we cleaned up. Then we saw Jesus. He was trying to talk to the people, but they were all crowding around Him. He looked up and seeing our boat, came over and simply got into it. He called to me with a smile, asking me to put out a little from shore so He could talk to the crowd. I did so gladly as both Andrew and I were glad to have the opportunity to hear Jesus teach again.

As soon as He'd finished speaking to the people, He looked straight at me and told me to put out into the deeper water and let down the nets for a catch! Well, we'd spent all night in the deep water waiting for a catch, but it had been one of those wasted nights. Anyway, we'd already washed the wretched nets up hadn't we? But there was something in His tone that made me tell Him so much more than I'd intended. I told Him what a dreadful night it had been, but then said because He had asked me to, I'd do it. After all, He'd been to my home, and I'd seen what He'd done. His power had healed my mum-in-law, healed all those people, even released the demon possessed, so it was worth a go, wasn't it?

I did as He had said and you may not believe this, but no sooner had I put down those nets in the water than they were full. When I say full, there was nearly a week's catch in the one! I yelled to Andrew, James and John to get themselves over to me to pull this catch in otherwise the net was going to break. There were so many fish, it nearly sank both our boats. It was a huge struggle, but we got to shore somehow.

That was the crunch point for me, I guess. I fell at the knees of this teacher-preacher man, Jesus. I knew goodness and power when I saw it. This guy was different from the usual teachers though. Goodness and authority seem to flow out of Him somehow.
What a catch of fish! I mean, how did He know where they were? We were the fishermen, the experts, yet we hadn't found any that night.
I told Him to go away from me, I know what I am, I'm not perfect at all. I'm a sinful man and I told Him so. I'm not sure what I expected Him to do, but despite this man having had such an effect on me, I didn't expect what He did say! He told me "Don't be afraid Simon Peter; from now on you will fish for people."

All four of us knew this was a life changing moment in all our lives. His call wasn't just to me, but to Andrew, James and John too. They were all as gobsmacked as I was at this phenomenal catch of fish, yet we knew that we had no real alternative but to draw up the boats and follow Jesus. To do anything else would have been unthinkable.
I don't think any of us, least of all me, knew what would lie ahead, I knew only that if I didn't go with Him, my life, our lives would have been as empty as the nets had been before we met Him. I knew I would forever regret it and that whatever my life would become from this moment on, it was what I was truly born to. Sounds melodramatic and perhaps daft, but this far from perfect fisherman wanted to know what it was to catch people with Jesus.

THROUGH THE ROOF

Alpheus was a great friend of ours, we'd been mates since childhood. He got into a bit of bother in his teenage years, so we kind of drifted apart a little although we still saw each other from time to time.

Eventually, when we had all settled down with our wives and families and the old group had gradually got back together again, we made a terrible discovery. Alpheus was paralysed and reduced to begging. None of us knew how this had happened, because as I said, he had drifted away from us for a bit and once we knew he was in this state, we didn't like to ask. We did what we could, giving him what we could spare, taking him to where he could beg and bringing him home again. The reality was though that for each of us it was like a knife through our hearts each time we saw him or had to lift his pallet and help him. We knew, because we'd known him for so many years, that he hated it too and in amongst his gratitude there was a resentment that this was how his life had turned out in comparison to ours. That was understandable. It was natural really. He never vocalised it, was always grateful, always laughed and joked with us, just as he'd always done, but we all knew that feeling was there, like a spectre, hovering just out of sight. The pallet we lifted him on was not just a support for his body but more like a straitjacket preventing him from being fully one of the old gang.

It was Joseph who first came and mentioned Jesus. He'd heard from his boss about this man who healed people. I don't just mean he stopped them feeling rough, I mean people who were blind being able to see again, deaf mutes able to hear and talk, those who had a demon in them being set free, lepers being healed. It was serious stuff!

We kept chatting about it and when we heard that this Jesus was coming to our town, the four of us decided that it was worth a shot for our friend. So, instead of taking him to the usual place for him to beg, this particular day we took him to where Jesus was. When we got there the crowd was immense. We hadn't thought that through. It was made worse by the fact that the Pharisees and all the teachers of the law had turned up to hear Him too, so all of them, together with all those who were following Jesus, plus all the rest of our town meant that it was impossible to get anywhere near Him. Alpheus, trying hard to not sound disappointed, but not quite managing it, told us not to worry and thanked us. He told us just to take him to his usual place to beg.

It's strange isn't it, 'life'? We'd all kind of thought the same thing, but as soon as Alpheus said it aloud, each of us felt determined not to give up. We'd come to see Jesus, so we were going to take Alpheus to see Him somehow or other.

Now Zach was a builder and he looked at this building and at Jesus and the massive crowd were in. He turned to me and said thoughtfully, clearly working it out in his mind as he went along, 'You know, if we went up on to the roof, we could chip away at the clay. It might take a while, but with the four of us, we should be able to remove the planks, so that we could then lower him down right in front of Jesus.'

Well, it seemed like a plan to us. We had a look through the crowd to see where Jesus was and with Zach's knowledge, he could work out where we needed to be on the roof, so up we went. Alpheus tried to protest, but not convincingly, the gratitude and hope shone out of his face that we hadn't given up on getting him to Jesus!

It took a long while and it wasn't easy in the blazing sun. I have no idea what the crowd thought beneath us as dust and bits began to fall. Gradually we began to faintly hear Jesus' voice and then a little later, after more work chipping away, we finally saw Him. Everyone was looking up, wondering what on earth we were doing. Everyone that was except Him, except Jesus. It might have been my imagination, or working in the sun for so long, but it seemed to me that He was waiting for us to finish what we had started!

After an incredibly long time, we finally had a hole large enough to lower Alpheus down very carefully in front of Jesus.

As we did this, Jesus looked up at us, full of compassion and love. I'd like to give you the words for that look, to try to explain it, but I simply can't! I know it might sound daft, but I will never, ever forget that look, and how it made me feel.

Jesus then looked at Alpheus and said 'Son, your sins are forgiven.' Seriously? I was on the verge of crying out to Him, 'Er, excuse me, that's not why we've gone to all this trouble you know.' But I remembered that expression of His from a few moments ago and all four of us waited.

The Pharisees and teachers of the law in the front row seats began squirming, they clearly weren't happy and started whispering to each other. Now I don't know if Jesus has super hearing or whether He knew what they muttered some other way, but He said "Why are you thinking these things? Which is easier, to say 'Your sins are forgiven' or 'Be healed'?" Then He looked directly at Alpheus, who somehow already looked ten years younger, looked better, looked, well more like he used to look. Jesus said, "So that you will all remember that the Son of Man has authority to forgive sins here on earth, I tell you, get up, take your mat and go home."

Before we could think much about this, there was Alpheus, standing. Actually, he was jumping and hollering, praising God, cheering as he looked up at us. We were utterly amazed, but delighted too and ran down the steps to see him outside the house as he pushed through the crowds to get to us.

'Son of Man' He called Himself. I don't know about that, but I do know that our mate Alpheus is a changed man. He's working with Zach now. The roof was fixed by both of them, so that it looks like new. Alpheus tells everyone who will listen about the day he was lowered through a roof paralysed yet ran from that house on the same day fully healed and forgiven.

I can tell you; he wasn't the only one whose life had been changed forever by it all!

THE WATER GIVING MESSIAH

My family all come from Sychar, we're known there. Like most women, I married young. My husband was a good man to begin with, but it didn't take long before became a wastrel really, drinking all day and rolling in drunk every night and I couldn't bear it. The inevitable happened one night as he was rolling home drunk from too much wine. He met with an accident and was killed. My second husband was lovely, but he contracted leprosy and died also. It wasn't so easy to find a third husband. Neither of their deaths were my fault, but when I married for the third time, I was seen as damaged goods & it was that I think which gave my husband the idea of issuing me with a certificate of divorce and the same became even more so the case with my fourth husband.

Anyway, it wasn't really the life I would have chosen, this life I had become accustomed to.

It was as if with each death and then each certificate of divorce, I withdrew further and further from normal society. I became the black pariah in our town - everyone knew of me, but no-one wanted to know me.

It was ok, this half-life, it wasn't a bad life and I had what I needed, or at least I thought I did. True, I couldn't go to the market with everyone else because they pointed the finger but going late to the market meant I got the bargains at the end of the day!

Going to get water from the well was the hardest really, because I had to go during the heat of the day to avoid the gossips and the slanderers.

Then, that day came! That day above all other days, the day when my life changed!

I'd gone, just as I did every day, it was about noon. As I got to the well there was a man there. I set myself to ignore him and steeled myself for some kind of verbal abuse, but as I drew closer, I realised He was a Jew. I didn't recognise Him at all, so I relaxed.
As I began to draw my water, He spoke to me - well, there was no-one else, so I knew He was speaking to me. He asked me to get Him a drink. Well, I was stunned on both counts - firstly that being a Jew, He would ask me, a Samaritan for a drink, but also that He, a Jewish man, would even speak to me, a Samaritan woman! You know how things are between Jews and Samaritans, Jews simply do not associate with us Samaritans!

He said something really strange then, He said that if only I'd known who it was that was asking for water, I'd ask Him to give me living water. Well, I just laughed then. Boy, did laughing feel good after all this time. He had no pitcher, nothing with which to draw water, yet He reckoned I should have been asking Him for a drink!
When I'd stopped laughing a little, I asked Him whether He thought He was greater than our forefather Jacob, (for it was at Jacob's well where I had met Him), that He could give me water?
It then got even more strange with this man from Galilee. He told me that everyone who drank of the water from Jacob's well would thirst again, but if you had some of His living water, you'd have your own wellspring inside and eternal life as well!
Well, who wouldn't want that eh? 'Sir,' I said, 'give me this living water, so I don't have to come here every day. I'd really like that!'
His next words shook me, quelling any remaining laughter and bringing me back to reality with a jolt. He asked me to go and call my husband!

Ah, now there was the problem. Yet, what was so strange was that I didn't think to lie, or give excuses; it didn't occur to me to do anything other than tell Him I had no husband.
If I'd been amused and surprised before, now, I was confounded.

He told me He knew I'd answered truly that He knew I'd had five husbands and the man I now lived with wasn't even my husband. You know that feeling when you don't know what to say and you find yourself burbling? Well, I began to burble at that point, telling Him I could see He was a prophet!
He spoke of there being a time coming where we wouldn't worship on this mountain or even in Jerusalem - not that we did that, of course. Well, everyone knows the stories from the Jews, even if we don't associate with them, don’t they? We know about the Messiah who would come from the Jews and explain everything. I don't know even now, what made me think of it, but I said that to Him.

I looked at Him, I mean looked at Him properly and He looked at me even more intently.
The world stopped.

He said, "I who am talking to you, I AM He."
I was astounded and the world which had seemed to have stopped spinning began to spin again. Was this truly the Messiah?

Out of the jumble of thoughts that had spun around in my head I realised then that actually I believed Him! I believed this stranger from Galilee, I believed I thought He was the Messiah and although I still don't fully understand why and I've never really been taught much about these things, I knew I had to tell other people that I'd met and spoken to Him, the Messiah.

I look back now and realise just how big a deal it was for me to tell people I had met with Jesus - yes, I know His name now. At the time though I was simply compelled to go and tell people that I'd met Him, that they should come to meet Him too.
I forgot that they wouldn’t normally talk to me. I forgot what I'd become. I forgot how they viewed me, and I went and told them I'd met this Galilean who had told me everything I'd ever done and that I thought He might be the Messiah and that they should come and see Him for themselves.

Well, they did come, and Jesus stayed around our town for a couple of days because there were so many people who wanted to ask Him questions. I listened to Him as He taught us all and life has never returned to that lonely place it was.

It never could, not when you've met the Messiah, the Saviour, Jesus! Nothing can ever go back to what was, for life is different once you have encountered Jesus.

THE WIDOW OF NAIN

I am proud of my son, I guess every mother is really. He's a good boy and cares for me. He is all I've got since my husband died and I am grateful to God, so grateful.

I remember the day so well when my son Caleb came home from his work with a fever. We thought nothing of it and I did what every mother does, giving him broth to soothe his throat and then made him comfortable. We both thought that the morning would see him improved.
I didn't sleep well that night, maybe in my heart I knew that this was more than a simple fever, I couldn't say. I do know that when I woke the next morning and began preparing his breakfast, there was no sign of him readying himself for the day. When I went into his room, I found he was worse, in fact he was delirious. I was so incredibly worried.

That day and all the next morning passed in a blur, people were coming and going as I had sent word of how ill he was and they came offering help and support. Along with family and neighbours I prayed so much that day, pleading with God for Caleb. God had taken my husband; would He now not spare me my son?

It was in the afternoon of the second day that Caleb died. The lament from those who were with me began and I was grateful for it. I had tears, but no strength to wail or lament, I was numb. The tears I shed came from somewhere within me beyond that numbness, somewhere I could feel the horror of my aloneness, even amidst friends and neighbours.

The time came for them to carry him out, there was quite a crowd. I dimly wondered why there were so many people and then HE appeared. He stepped forward and touched the bier. We all stopped, and I looked up at Him. I knew this had to be Jesus, the teacher people had spoken of, the one who healed.
He told me not to weep and somehow even as He said those words, hope began to fill me, because those few words were spoken with a love and compassion deeper than I had ever felt or experienced before.

I didn't have time to ponder why I felt hope, because the next words He spoke were to my son, my dead son, Caleb! He spoke directly to him, as though He were waking him in the morning, telling him to rise for a new day, He told him to rise up from death.

Caleb sat up, on his own funeral bier and spoke to Jesus, just like that! He knew it was Jesus who had brought him back to life, he recognised Him, and praised and thanked God. Then he jumped down from the bier and Jesus gave him back to me. He really did, in every way give my Caleb back to me.

How quickly can the despairing numbness of grief turn to joy? As quickly as the man, Jesus from Galilee speaks the words of life "Rise up!" That's how quickly!

THE MAN WHO CALMED THE SEA

My life has changed so much recently. Have you ever had those times in your life where everything seems to just jog along, then something happens and life changes completely, by simply meeting someone?
Well, it happened to me.
I was introduced to a man called Jesus, who had called my friends Peter, James and John to be his followers. When I heard his teaching, I wanted to be a follower too. It was like my life up to that point had been lived in monochrome and suddenly it was filled with the most glorious colours you could ever imagine. He taught us things about life, about worrying, about judging people, about all kinds of things and what he said didn't just make sense, it fitted together in a way that things I'd heard beforehand just didn't seem to do!

After I began to follow him, I didn't just hear, but also saw some amazing things. I saw a man healed of leprosy! Completely cured, instantly, by Jesus. Then there was the servant of a centurion who was healed with simply a word from Jesus, He didn't even need to go and see the guy! Then, Peter's mum-in-law was ill – Jesus healed her so quickly she was well enough to serve us dinner!
Nothing prepared me for what happened just now though. He'd told the crowds we were going over to the other side of the lake. We all got in the boat with him, as usual. It was Andrew and Peter's boat, a sturdy fishing boat like many others, which was plenty big enough for all of us.

We'd not got out very far when one of those storms rose up which happen on the Sea of Galilee – the ones you get no warning of but are so ferocious you vow never, ever to get in a boat again. This was one of those storms. It seemed the boat had shrunk in proportion to the size of the waves which engulfed us, going right over the boat. I just followed what Peter and Andrew told me to do, we all did, well, I say all, but as I looked over to where we'd been sitting, I saw Jesus, fast asleep. Honestly, how could anyone possibly sleep through these kinds of winds and waves? I don't know, but sleep He did!

None of us had time to think about it very long, but someone vocalised what we were all thinking and went to wake Jesus, shouting, 'Haven't you seen this storm? Don't you care that we're drowning?' Whatever I expected Jesus to say and do, I can tell you it was not what He said and did! His first words were ones of rebuke, 'Oh you of little faith, why do you doubt?'. Personally, I wasn't at all sure what faith had to do with being caught in a storm and facing death, but I didn't have much time to think about it because His next two words, 'Be still' transformed everything.

The storm just stopped. Completely.
No wind, not even so much as a breeze. The waves, merely ripples on the side of the boat, and the evening sun breaking through the clouds. We all simply looked at each other, at the sea, at Jesus and at each other again. We were amazed, yes, but more than that, we were afraid. We began to ask who this man was? Who can command the wind and waves to stop and have them they do so immediately?

He saved our lives, no doubt about it, but I'm not sure now where I go from here with this Jesus. He is scary, wonderful, but scary nonetheless. All I know is that I can't walk away from Him. I can't pretend life with Jesus isn't likely to be the most amazingly daunting, unpredictable journey. It's probably all that and more, but I do know I couldn't, wouldn't want to be anywhere else, with anyone else or doing anything else than what I am doing with

Jesus, for I am a friend, more than that, I am a disciple of the Man who calmed the sea!

THE PIG-KEEPER, THE TOMB MAN AND THE PEACE-GIVER

I used to keep pigs! It's not a job anyone else wants really. I was not envied in any way, because where I come from, the people around me will have nothing to do with pigs and see them as unclean. I quite liked my pigs. They are sociable creatures, affectionate and not as filthy as people think them to be.
I was happy enough with my life, living in the Gerasenes, a fairly remote part of Judea. The only other person who lived near me was a guy who was, quite frankly out of his mind. He lived among the tombs and he often ran around screaming at the top of his voice. He broke all the chains with which the authorities tried to bind him to keep him and everyone else safe and he ran away from all who would try to seek him out. His nickname was 'tomb man'. He left me alone, never tried to attack me, even in his tortured mind there was something he saw which recognised I wasn't a threat. I liked to think he saw in me someone who was an outcast, just as he was.

One day, actually THE day, a guy I'd never seen before got out of a fishing boat nearby with a small group I assumed were his friends. There was nothing really unusual in that, people did it all the time. What made this different though was that it was a fishing boat, not one of the usual boats that carried people across to our part of the world. Anyway, they walked towards me, but were halted by 'tomb man'! I thought he was going to attack them

like he normally did. I used to fade into the background when this happened. After all, we might exist peaceably together most of the time, but I have never interfered or tried in any way to restrain him and wasn't going to start doing so, because I knew it was useless to try.
He yelled at them as he always did, but this time he was actually making something akin to sense! That baffled me to be honest. He often screamed, but usually most of his words were words of foul abuse which offfended those who came to restrain him. It no longer shocked me because I was accustomed to it, but this was different. What he shouted stunned me as much as the foul language scandalized others because it was such a change from the norm!

He yelled "What do you want with me, Jesus, Son of the Most High God? I beg you, don't torture me!"

I was so surprised; I came out from where I'd been hiding. I was so dumbfounded. A coherent sentence from this man who mumbled all the time and spouted gibberish and abuse most of the time when anyone came near him, yet here he was, sounding, well not 'normal', but he was, at least, making sense! I had to look and see who it was he was speaking to, because there had to be something different about whoever it was who had drawn a fully formed sentence from 'tomb man'.
When I looked at this person, Jesus, who had provoked this reaction, He didn't look any different to the others He was with. There was nothing in the way He looked that would make Him stand out in a crowd, yet there was something about Him that was different, peculiar, unique even.
Then, He spoke!

He said to 'tomb man,' "What is your name?" I almost laughed aloud at that point, because no-one knew his name, he was simply 'tomb man', but something in this man, this Jesus, stopped me. Don't ask me how, but I realised that Jesus wasn't talking to 'tomb man', but to something, or someone else.

'Tomb man' spoke again. "We are legion, but we beg you, do not cast us into the abyss. We beg you to send us into that herd of pigs!"
Well, you can imagine how horrified I was at this and was just about to do what I never do and speak up. After all, the pigs are my livelihood – who knows what would happen if what was inside 'tomb man' went into my pigs? Before I'd had a chance to do anything, Jesus gave this 'legion' permission to go into my pigs!

It all happened so very quickly then; my pigs began to run around nipping at each other and running towards the cliff by the sea. Then, before I could do or say anything, they'd run off the cliff, into the sea. They were gone. Every last one of them, gone!

I know it may sound silly, but all I remember after that was the silence and the peace. It took me a little time, my thoughts were so jumbled, to work out what it was that was so surprised me. After a while I suddenly realised that 'tomb man' was still. 'Tomb man' wasn't mumbling, screaming, or making any noise at all. 'Tomb man' was on the ground, sitting up and looking around him as though he was seeing everything for the very first time. His eyes then fixed on Jesus, and he knelt before Him.

The voice I then heard coming from 'tomb man', (actually I need to call him Simon, as now I know that is his name), wasn't like the voice I had heard coming from him before, it was a normal voice. A gentle, soft voice. This voice spoke and the man to whom it belonged looked into Jesus' face and thanked Him for setting him free.

I had to think quickly, and to be honest, wanted to get away swiftly. After all, what would the owners of the pigs say when they knew that they had just thrown themselves off the cliff into the sea and were drowned? I ran to the village. People stopped and they listened to me, I think that was because they knew who I was and knew it had to be something quite important for me to be running and shouting the way I was.

I told them what had happened. I told them that 'tomb man' was sitting and talking like any one of us. I told them that the pigs had run into the sea, and were all drowned, that Jesus had spoken to whatever 'legion' it was that had been inside 'tomb man' and that it had gone into the pigs and this was what had caused them to do that. The owners of the pigs wanted to come and see this Jesus and have words with Him. The rest of the village would, I knew follow him, for it is not every day something like this happens.

When we returned, Simon was still talking to Jesus, just as any one of us would talk with a friend. It seemed that Jesus' friends had some clothes in their boat, because Simon too was clothed and clearly in his right mind. I didn't need to say anything more to the owners of the pigs, they could see something miraculous had happened here. There was still that sense of peace I had felt earlier, even amidst the hustle and bustle of the townsfolk. I think they felt something too as the elders of the town spoke directly to Jesus and begged Him to leave our town. He was altogether too unpredictable, frightening, and unexplainable.

I was a little sad because there was something in Him that attracted me. I was never particularly impressed with people. I guess that's why I became a pig-keeper, so I could stay away from people, but this Jesus was different. Simon asked to go with Jesus, but Jesus told him to stay and tell the people all around the area what He had done for him and how he had been healed and restored to his right mind. Simon accepted that. I had nothing to stay for, as his story wasn't mine to tell really, it was rightly Simon's. I plucked up courage to ask Jesus if I could come with Him. He turned to talk to me, and I could see in His eyes that peace which had so impacted me earlier, and He smiled. He told me that He'd come to free both Simon and me and that I could and would follow Him all my life.

He was right on all counts.

SIGHT BROUGHT ON THE SABBATH

I was born blind which meant that I grew up with the inherited stigma my parents felt about having a son who had been born blind.

They felt somehow that they must have sinned against God for this to happen. They love me, I know they do, but I also know without ever seeing their faces that every time they looked at me, or when I was older helped me to my place to beg, they were reminded of what they saw as their sin. It was never named, this 'sin', but like the runt of the litter of pups, I was cared for, I was loved by them, but I was also a constant source of embarrassment. There are, you see, some things you instinctively understand. You don't need eyes that can see, to know them.

One Sabbath day, everything changed; and yes, I mean everything. When you beg, as I had done for many years, you learn to listen intently to some conversations, but filter out others which aren't as interesting or important.
On this particular day, I heard a group of men walking and talking together discussing the world, as men are inclined to do. My ears pricked up as I heard one ask of another 'Teacher, who sinned as this man was born blind?'
Here we go, I thought, I wish my parents were here to hear this discussion! Then, the Teacher spoke..... I knew He had to be the Teacher for I'd not heard anyone speak with the weight of authority that this guy did. I had a clear picture of Him in my mind....He was probably a Pharisee, I decided, so He would have

nothing to do with the likes of me, the dregs of society. He spoke about 'doing the work of God whilst it was still light, because darkness would come soon.'

Without making any audible sound, I laughed. My life was full of darkness. Yes, I could feel the heat of the sun and the difference with the coolness of the evening when the sun goes down, but light and dark? They were both the same to me. Still, I was interested to hear His reply to their query, well lets be honest, that question had followed me throughout my life.

His reply, and everything about Jesus, for that was His name, astounded me. I remembered then that I had heard many others talk of Him, this 'healer from Galilee' who worked miracles. He said to those following Him, 'Neither this man, nor his parents sinned, that isn't even the right question to ask! No, he was born blind that the glory of God might be seen through him.'

Well, what can you say in response to that? It left me with more questions than my brain had room to ask, but before either the men with Him, or I could ask any further questions, I heard someone spit on the ground.

I was grateful they'd missed me this time and expected everyone would move on and I would unfortunately miss the rest of the discussion, but a few seconds later I felt someone touch my eyes and spread something on them. Then I heard Him, Jesus that is, speak again to me! He told me to go and wash in the pool called Sent. Well, I wasn't far from it, I knew of it, and I'd drunk from it, but didn't go too near it for if my helpers had to leave me, I didn't want to fall into it, so the place from which I begged was some distance from it.

People helped me to the pool and I knelt, feeling for the water which was deliciously cool despite the heat of the day. I washed off what felt like drying clay from my eyes and when I had done so, you won't believe what had happened, I could see the sunlight on the ripples of water. I could see people around me and I could see them watching me.

I COULD SEE!

My helpers, neighbours and friends could hardly believe it. Some who didn't know me well said I wasn't really the man born blind who used to beg just over there. I could look at them, I could see them, and I told them, 'Yes, I am the guy who used to beg over there, I was born blind, but look, I can see.'
I know my whole face was alight with the smile that radiated from somewhere deep within me, but how could I not be filled with joy, I was blind, now I could see.
I told them the truth 'The man they call Jesus got some mud, put it on my eyes and told me to go wash in the Sent pool and when I did, I could see!' They wanted to know where He was, but I hadn't heard Him since I had washed in the pool, so I couldn't tell them.

They all decided I should go to the Pharisees, well I was still a bit dazed, as I thought this Jesus might be with them, so that's where I went. They asked me the same question about how I had received my sight, so I told them the same thing 'He put mud on my eyes and told me to go and wash. I did and then I could see!'
I still didn't hear the voice of Jesus anywhere as they began discussing amongst themselves as to whether He was a sinner because He had healed on the Sabbath day. I remember thinking that surely a Sabbath day was the best day of all to be bringing glory to God and worshipping Him, which I was now doing as joy indescribable was filling me.

Finally, they turned to talk to me, I could see them turn. You won't understand what a joy that is, I didn't just hear the rustling of robes, the sense of movement, I could see them turn and look at me. They asked me then, 'What do you say about Him?' 'Well,' I answered, 'He must at the very least be some sort of prophet.'
They continued arguing as I watched and listened to them. What they were saying seemed so utterly trivial. Could they not see, these people who had always had sight, did they not realise that I was blind and now I could see?
Still, they discussed and argued about whether I had actually been

blind. I wanted to laugh, but then they brought in my parents.
I saw them for the first time. They looked older than I'd imagined, smaller somehow, weighed down by, well, I don't know what. They looked fearful, bless them.

The Pharisees asked them, 'Is this your son? Are you seriously telling us he was born blind? How is it then that he can now see?' My heart lurched as I looked at my poor bemused parents, so scared that their hard won standing in the community should be lost by saying they believed in Jesus' healing power because they could see the result of it in their own son.

I remembered then that people had said the Pharisees would ban from the synagogue anyone who declared they believed His teaching. I felt deeply for these people who had loved and cared for me, their son, despite all the pain my blindness had caused them. I wanted them to meet Jesus, to hear what He had said before He healed me.
They were scared and indeed their reply showed just how scared, but even in their answer they showed they knew I had been healed by a miracle. They assured the Pharisees that I was their son, but that for anything else, to ask me, I was of age, and it wasn't for them to answer for me. I admired them for that reply, for it showed their faith in me to give an answer.

The Pharisees then asked me to tell the truth about what had happened saying now that they knew this Jesus to be a sinner! I simply told them 'I don't know whether He is a sinner, what I do know and am telling you the truth. I was blind, now, I can see!'

They asked again how He had opened my eyes? By this time, I was getting a little perplexed. Why did these learned men of God keep asking the same question?
I replied 'I've told you a number of times what happened. Why do you want to hear it yet again? Do you want to follow Him too?' I simply couldn't see why they couldn't understand.

I hadn't expected the anger and the venom with which they

responded. I'd known what it was being spat at before, but that was in derision, this was different, more sinister somehow. They spat their words to me in fury 'You must be one of His disciples, we are disciples of our father Moses. We know God spoke to Moses, but where this Jesus bloke is from, we have no idea!'
How could they say that? How could they not know? He had given this blind man the gift of sight, He had brought light into my dark world, He had brought freedom to my life, how could they then not know where He was from? How could anyone who was a sinner do the things that only God Himself can do? Whoever heard of a man being born blind yet made to see? It couldn't be anything other than the power of God, could it?

Their final retort simply made me laugh. They instructed I be thrown out of the synagogue 'Surely he was steeped in sin at birth, get him out of here!' They thought they had all the answers, they were teachers, yet they knew nothing. My parents didn't need to fear them, they were fools who although not blind as I had been for so many years were nonetheless grovelling in a darkness far worse than mine had been, for they couldn't see what was standing in front of them!
As I went from the synagogue into the sunlight, I'd never realised how gloriously golden sunlight is and how it illuminates all it touches, I saw Him! I realised then that I didn't need to hear Him, I knew it was Him.

He asked me whether I believed in the Son of Man. I found myself replying 'Tell me who He is Sir, that I may believe'. As I said those words, I knew what He would say, who He really was. So, I was not surprised when Jesus said "You have now seen Him; in fact, He is the one speaking with you."
I knew it, guessed it, realised it, so when He spoke those words to me, I simply bowed down before Him and worshipped. What else was there to do?
This was the Messiah. He was God's Son of Man and He had done what the prophet of old had said the Messiah would do. With

all my newfound sight I had only dimly glimpsed before that moment that He had brought freedom for this captive, sight for this blind man, joy instead of mourning, a cloak of praise instead of a spirit of despair.

THE LIFTER OF MY HEAD

I'd lost everything.

Well, everything that meant anything to me. My husband was an upright man who feared God, and kept the law, so could have nothing to do with me. If you know the law of Moses, you would know I am unclean because of my illness. We lived in the same house, but that was all there could be and all there had been for 12 years. Twelve long, draining years.

To begin with we had tried. The doctors had attempted so many different treatments, but eventually each would shake their heads, look at my husband with sadness and pity but with no idea of how to cure me.

So, life went on.

I'd heard about Jesus. Someone I knew told me that He was coming to our town. I remember wondering, but that wonder was followed by another unusual feeling that grew inside me and I couldn't shut it out of my mind. It grew and wouldn't be silenced, 'If I just touch the hem of His cloak....I don't need to bother Him, or even say why I am doing it. I don't need to draw attention to myself.'

Think about it. I shouldn't be out in public, I certainly shouldn't be in a crowd where anyone would be made unclean by touching me, even inadvertently. Surely, He wouldn't have anything to do with me if I said what was wrong. I couldn't speak my problem out loud, being unclean as I am and I somehow just couldn't deal with that on top of everything else.

But I could go, I could just touch His cloak. That way no-one need ever know, but I would be healed.

I'm not sure how or even why I was so sure. Like I said, it was a conviction that wouldn't go away, it wouldn't be assuaged, ironically just like my problem!

So, the day came, I joined the crowd, gradually working my way forward towards Jesus. His disciples couldn't keep people from Him, but that suited my one overriding purpose....to touch His cloak.

Gradually and after many false starts where I got jostled by someone, I began to get closer. I got closer and closer, and then, I did it, I touched His cloak!

The world stood still for a minute as the crowd carried on without me. I stood still because I knew I'd been healed. It's hard to describe, but I simply knew deep within my body, mind, and heart that it was over, that I was healed. I knew it every bit as undoubtedly as I had known I would be once I touched His cloak. It was at this point I realised that the crowd had stopped moving and Jesus was asking a question.

'Who touched my cloak?'

My heart was in my mouth, I knew He must mean me.

He knew! I didn't know how, but He certainly knew what I'd done. He looked around, over heads, until His gaze began to move towards me, and I knew I would have to speak up. I would have to say it was me, but I in reality, all I wanted was to just run away home, clean and healed.
I was terrified but fell at His feet. The pain, anguish and the upset of the last twelve years poured out of me as I told Him how I'd just known that if I touched His cloak, I'd be healed, and I was healed! He had healed me.
He bent down and lifted my head, oh so gently and tenderly. The look of love and acceptance in His eyes was so powerful it swept away all fear and worry.

Then, He spoke words which will stay with me forever: 'Daughter, your faith and trust in Me has healed you. Go now, don't fear this will return, simply continue in your healing.'
I can't explain just how His words and His manner toward me had become life defining for me, greater potentially even than being healed, or it seemed so to me right then. For the first time in my life, I knew who I was and that I mattered.

Now, I have my life back. Where before there was pain and isolation, where I kept my head down, now, it was as though sunshine and brightness had entered into my life. When He had lifted my head, it was as if He had affirmed who I am. I could hold my head high now; I could live life to the full. In the Scriptures King David wrote, 'He is my glory and the lifter of my head.' I claim that for I know it to be true. He was, is and always will be.

TWO BLIND BEGGARS

It seemed I'd waited for this day all my life. I was with Reuben, as usual. We tended to stick together, and we'd spoken much about Jesus and about what we had heard about Him being able to heal and restore sight, as well as much more. Well, really we didn't care about the much more, but we certainly cared about being able to see! The problem for us both was that neither of us had any family who would take us to Jesus, and we only had each other as friends – who else wants to be a friend of a blind man who sits begging all day?

Anyway, we'd decided that the only way to get His attention the next time He came into our town, was to shout and scream until He heard us. What was it we should shout though? We needed Him to know we believed in who He says He is, so after much discussion we decided we'd shout 'Adonai, Lord, have mercy on us, oh Son of David, have mercy'.

We knew we had to time it just right you see, we knew we had to shout it in unison, in order for Him to hear us above the crowd. He was unlikely to see us – most people don't. We fade into the background of their lives, just part of the scenery.

We heard the crowd surrounding Jesus long before they arrived. We waited and waited until we both knew it was THE time. We yelled as loud as we possibly could, in unison, in our overwhelming desire for this one chance at healing. 'Adonai, Lord, have mercy on us, oh Son of David, have mercy'.

The first thing that happened was that the crowd must have seen us, they certainly heard us because they told us to be still and shut up! They didn't think Jesus wanted to be bothered with the likes of us – blind beggars, part of the distasteful side of life. Reuben and I didn't care, we yelled again, louder this time because we were scared. We couldn't let this one chance pass us by, we just couldn't allow that to happen.

'Adonai, have mercy on us, oh Son of David, have mercy'.
We heard that the crowd had stopped moving. My heart seemed to stop with the crowd as an eternity passed and we waited to see what would happen next.
What actually happened was that He called us, HE called us by name. He didn't just call out 'Hey you two blind beggars' He called our names. We helped each other up, as we always did and then some of the people in the crowd took us the few steps over to Him. We knew it was Him when He asked us what we wanted Him to do for us – there is something in His voice you know, a kind of gentle power that you couldn't argue with!

We told Him we simply wanted to see. It's everything we ever wanted, just to be able to have our eyes opened.
Next thing I knew, Reuben gave a shout, 'I can see, I can see!' But before I had time to wonder or to think anything any longer, I felt a touch on my eyes; such a light touch with such heat, which permeated right through my eyes and into my whole being, like the sun in all its strength warming me in my whole body. Suddenly I was aware; I could feel my eyes. I could open them. I could see!

Reuben and I hadn't thought beyond being healed, hadn't thought about what we'd do if we were healed, but neither of us felt any doubts after we had been healed, no discussion was needed, there was no question once we were able to see. No question because all we could do was worship Him and follow Him. Our sight wasn't everything as we'd thought, because ultimately it turns out He was and is everything!

WALKING ON WATER? REALLY!

We were out in the boat, you know, at that dark time just before dawn. There wasn't a storm, but it was pretty windy. On the Sea of Galilee there is a difference and I'd been in boats for all my life, so had seen both, believe me! There were however lots of 'white horses' on the lake. We were used to it; Andrew and I had grown up being tossed about in a fishing boat since being quite small.

The twelve of us were there, Jesus had gone to pray – another all-nighter, but we were used to Him doing that. He told us that He spent the time talking to His Father. It was clearly a precious time for Him, and we didn't know quite what we'd do if we followed Him there and as He hadn't invited us, we left Him to it.

It was quite late, or early, depending on your point of view when we saw something out on the water coming towards us, something light, but not 'a' light, just lighter than the darkness we expected. As we stared at it, trying to focus our eyes against the wind, we all agreed; 'It looks like Jesus.' '...But that would be ridiculous, wouldn't it?' 'Don't be silly, that would mean, well..........' He was talking to His Father on the shore and we had taken the boat.

We kept staring, wondering what it could be? Some sort of spirit maybe, a trick of the light, yet it looked just like Him! The closer He got, the more like Jesus it looked. Someone in the boat called out to the figure, well, we were a bit spooked by this point. A voice answered, the voice we all knew and recognized. It WAS Jesus!

He told us not to be afraid and said, 'I AM' He used that name – that precious unspeakable name. Well, that shook us all, but for me it was only in that way that you'd known something, but not completely known it. You'd just fallen short of fully realizing it. At that point it made perfect sense to me, If He really was the Messiah, the chosen of God, of course He could walk on water, He can do whatever He likes. Didn't Moses do miraculous signs in the power of God, didn't Elijah call down fire from heaven? If they could do that by the power of God, why couldn't the Messiah, the Chosen One of God walk on water?

I decided I wanted to see what it was like to walk on water, so I called out that if it really was Jesus, He could ask me to come to Him. I knew it had to be Him – who else could it be? He called me, just like He'd called me to leave my fishing nets, He called me to leave the safety of the boat. I stepped out on to the water, it felt funny – like being in a boat made of tarpaulins. I began to walk to Him, keeping Him in my gaze, until one of those white horse waves lapped over my feet and my legs and I freaked out – my mind dimly realizing that if that had happened it meant I was beginning to sink.

At that point I was terrified I was going to die – Why do I always do stupid things like this? I should have stopped and thought before I got out of the boat – I'm a fisherman, I can't walk on water for goodness' sake. I screamed out to Jesus in terror.

I must have been nearer to Him than I thought because He reached out His hand and I was safe. I was standing next to Him on the water. He told me I shouldn't have doubted and asked what I was afraid of? Somehow, I couldn't state the obvious, (Er, the waves, walking on water, sinking, drowning etc.) because He was still holding my hand and nothing in all of creation was as safe as Him holding on to my hand. I began to ask myself the same question, 'Why had I freaked?' He was there, there wasn't any need to freak or fear with His right hand holding mine!

We climbed back into the boat, but I was more subdued by this point, trying to assimilate just what had happened, but also with the knowledge that I knew for certain who Jesus was. Only the Messiah, the chosen of God could walk on water, yet He had done that and called me to Him. I walked on water by His power. What else could He do and what else could we do through this power?

A BRUSH WITH TRUE AUTHORITY

I know I am despised. No-one who does what I do can avoid that. You are seen, by your own people as a collaborator, because you collect the taxes from the Romans. It is also 'expected' by both the Romans and acknowledged by the people that you syphon off some of what you receive to line your own pockets. This I have done over many years – everyone I know does it; it's how we make our fortune.

I have a fortune now, I am a chief tax-collector, I have reached the pinnacle of my chosen career, but far from it being the delight it promised to be, it is hollow. I have everything money can buy, yet in reality I have nothing of any worth at all.

Obviously, I had heard of Jesus, who hadn't? I had heard of the miracles, of the teaching laced with authority and I admit, I was intrigued. Authority is a strange thing you see, I have authority over servants and minions who work for me, but within my heart I know I am only a pretender. I was intrigued to see true authority. So, when I heard He was coming to Jericho, the opportunity was too good to miss really.
I decided to take some time out and simply observe Him, watch Him, see what real authority looked like. I hadn't really bargained for the crowds though. I obviously should have done, but I didn't. But I hadn't got where I was without ingenuity and the ability to think round a problem, so I ran on ahead of the crowd and enjoyed again my boyhood delight of climbing up a Sycamore tree. It is amazing how freeing that simple act was. It is as though when I

climbed, the years fell away and my life was before me again, as in my youth and joy at both my ingenuity in outwitting the crowd and my hiddenness from them was intoxicating!

Nearer and nearer they came, He was in the midst of them with people all around Him, clamouring for His attention, for healing, for a touch to bring a blessing in their lives. Nearer and nearer and all the time I watched; I observed this man of influence. He truly is a man of authority. When you have spent your life emulating something, you know when you see and are confronted with the genuine article and in every sense that was what Jesus was!
The crowd stopped.
He stopped.
Right under the place where I was.
I stopped breathing, although I didn't realise, I was holding my breath. He looked straight up at me. Others followed His gaze and were surprised by seeing me, but He wasn't. He knew I was there; He'd always known I'd be there you see. True insight and authority.

He looked straight at me and said 'Zacchaeus, I'm coming to your house, come down from your hiding place, come down and change those things which you know you need to and want to change in your life.'
If you ever come upon someone who speaks with that kind of authority, you do not hesitate. I scrambled down that tree with the same absence of dignity as that of an adolescent, because that was how I felt in His presence. He knew my name..... He knew my emptiness..... He knew my heart's desire.

He came into my house and ate with us, drank with us. That was the moment my life changed. It couldn't but change. You can't come into contact with genuine power, genuine insight, genuine authority and have it leave you unchanged.
All the townsfolk were incensed at His coming to eat with me at my house and it was at that point I realised that they had no idea

how changed I was by my encounter with Him.

I stood, as one does on these occasions, but as I began to speak about giving back to the poor half of what I owned and of making good on any and every crooked dealing that had robbed anyone, the murmuring stopped. They looked at me strangely and I felt.....well, I felt a minuscule sense of hearing authority in my own voice! Not the sham authority I had spouted most of my adult life which had, for all those years covered over my insecurity, but a standing tall authority which emulated His!
I looked at Him when I realised this and saw in His eyes and in His smile that He knew this too. In response, He declared to my neighbours and townsfolk, 'Today salvation has come to this household, for a true son of Abraham has been reborn to be his true self. For I have come that what has been lost might be found.'

I knew better than anyone the truth of those words, for He had restored to me the ability to be who I really am and stop being the actor I had pretended all my adult life to be.
That's the difference authentic authority makes.

DESPAIR TO HOPE BY WAY OF LOVE

My life hasn't been easy. My father was cruel to me after my mother died and I grew up in a household of men, with four brothers. Each of them learned well from my father how to be cruel and life wasn't easy. I was pledged to be married to a friend of my fathers who seemed to be honourable, but who used me, then cast me aside when he had finished by breaking off our wedding. My father disowned me, assuming there was something in me that had caused his friend to discard me, and I did the only thing I could do, I fell into a life of prostitution. After all, I reasoned, men had used me all my life and been cruel to me, I may as well be paid for it.

So my life went on, from year to year, a relentless, grey sameness, on and on. It had become simply an existence, not a life I led, and I thought nothing could or would ever change, that I deserved no less and certainly no more.

I hadn't bargained for meeting Jesus.

I'd been on the periphery of various crowds following him when I had first seen Him. It wasn't just that I had seen Him, but that, despite my being where I always tried to be, in the background, He had seen me. That was what was the undoing of me.

Once He'd seen me, He'd held my eyes and there was something in His look, something different to every other man I had ever seen, or who had ever looked at me. Men normally look at me like I am a piece of meat with which they satiate their appetite, but they never truly see me. He'd looked at me and in that one look had seen into my very soul, yet though He had seen everything I am, there

wasn't condemnation or loathing, but acceptance and what I knew, despite never having experienced it, there was love.
I think it was that which made me go back again and again, each time I knew He was going to be in town. He had become a magnificent obsession for me from that one look. There had been other looks since that first one, each looking deeper and deeper into the fabric of who I really am, ignoring what others think of me. Each look drew me more and more. The compassion, sorrow, love and acceptance in His gaze drew me irresistibly like a moth to a flame.
Then I heard He was going to dinner at Simon's house. I knew Simon and Simon knew me, so did his servants, so I was able to get through the crowds there. I took my jar of perfume with me, for I knew what it was I wanted to do. He was reclining at the table and much talking was going on – Jesus spoke as He always did, answering their questions and asking them questions they couldn't answer.

As I sat at His feet the tears began. I unstopped the bottle of perfume to pour over His feet and as I did so it was like the uncorking of all my life, all the cruelty, the using and abusing poured out of me in tears as I poured that perfume over His feet. I remember well the moment I realised that although I had brought the perfume, I had forgotten a towel to wipe it away, so did the only thing I could do and let down my hair and wiped His feet with it and as I did so, I began to kiss His feet to pour out some of the love and gratitude I felt towards Him.
It was strange because although I knew they were all beginning to look at me, becoming aware of what it was I was doing, especially as I let down my hair, nevertheless, I knew that where I was, in this place, at His feet was the safest place I had ever been in my life and I had no worries. There were so many tears, on and on through the years of heartbreak, I'd never allowed myself to cry like that before.
Suddenly I became aware of Simon mumbling to himself. That wasn't unusual, but I also saw that Jesus was speaking to him.

He began to tell Simon one of His stories, His parables. I stopped crying to listen to Him talk of debts and of debtors, of one man who owed much money and of another who owed little, though neither could pay. When they were absolved from their debt Jesus asked, which would love more. Simon answered that it was the one who had been forgiven more, but you could tell he didn't know what Jesus was talking about and so was irritated.

Then, Jesus turned to me, looking straight at me, and told Simon that I had been washing His feet, kissing His feet, anointing His feet. Jesus knew the perfume I had used was costly, but He knew too that what I had done in full view of Simon and of all those people was just as costly.

Time stood still and my heart stopped as He looked straight into me and told me that my sins were forgiven because of the great love I had shown. My sins, all of them, every seedy, filthy, perverted sin, He knew them all yet they were forgiven by Him in that one moment. That one moment that changed the course of my life and set me free from my former existence to live my life as it should be lived. He had turned all my despair into hope.

TRANSFIGURED!

Jesus invited us, Peter, James and me, to go up with Him on the mountainside to pray. Although we were all tired, I was delighted for I truly wanted to know just how He prayed and how He drew such strength from His Father through those times. Yet, that wasn't what actually happened.
We climbed up the mountain together, but then Jesus moved away from us. As He drew away a little distance, I was aware of that kind of tingling you get when there is almost a spark of anticipation (it comes more often being with Jesus than it ever did before) that crackle of being infinitely in the present moment and being in the presence of God.

I looked up at Jesus and as I did so, it was as though He was being clothed from head to toe in light, but not light as we would normally see it. This light had a luminous quality and a brightness and clarity to it that wasn't of the earth. It didn't hurt my eyes in any way, yet it was the brightest of lights I had ever seen. Jesus was utterly transformed. It was still Jesus, but more than Jesus. He was brighter, bigger, totally majestic and awe-inspiring. All His features became more than they were, it's hard to put into words, but His eyes were terrifyingly beautiful and powerful, even more than usual. You knew He would be able to see into the very depths of your heart if He were to look at you. His face looked just like the sun in all it's splendour and the three of us were bathed in the light from Him, a light which transformed us just as sunlight transforms that which it touches in its radiance.

As we watched and my eyes became used to seeing this light streaming from Him, I saw that there were two others with Him. I thought to begin with it might have been James and Peter as I had been so wrapped up in this scene before me, but they were just as absorbed by it all as I was. None of us were sleepy anymore!

As I looked more closely, I saw that it appeared to be Moses and Elijah who were with Jesus, speaking to Him in a way that showed that they had clearly known Him so deeply and so well. I guessed that was only to be expected. Yet even in this, I just knew this was a new thing we were seeing, a culmination and a bringing together of both the Torah and Prophetic teaching. Not a superseding, but a glorious marriage of them both and also, it seemed to me, of all history up to this very moment.

They looked as though they were about to leave when Peter then got up and said he'd build a shelter for the three of them and for us to stay there. I understood what he wanted and why he wanted to stay there, because it was the kind of place and sight that you could gaze on forever and never become bored with. I also knew that there was no way this was going to happen, no way Jesus would allow this and no way this was something that you could stay simply looking at. Just as Peter had finished speaking a glorious cloud began to descend on the three of them and on us. There was a kind of substance and weight to this cloud, which I can't really explain and I knew that this was what our fathers had seen as they journeyed in the wilderness. This was the cloud of the glorious presence of God!
I was enthralled and then came the Voice!

The Voice of God.

We heard the voice of God speaking!

That was it, we couldn't watch any more. We were flat on our faces in awe, fear, reverence, amazement – too much to explain in mere human words. We heard Him say 'This is My Son, My Beloved, with Whom I am and have always been delighted. Listen to Him!'

We were hearing the very Voice of the Almighty. We were disciples following the Beloved of The Lord. My mind struggled with the fullness of all we had seen and experienced and time stood still......

The next thing I remember was hearing the voice of Jesus. You know, now I realise the reason He always spoke with power is because His voice was like His Father's voice and carried that same authority. When I looked up, it was simply the Jesus we had known and loved, telling us not to be afraid. I realised then that the terror we had felt was a holy terror, not like fear in the human sense, but a different kind of fear. Jesus was as He had always been and yet, I certainly couldn't see Him in the same way as before we had been up that mountainside and seen what we had seen and heard what we had heard.

Peter and James asked Him questions about Elijah coming before the Christ and I simply listened to them all, as everything Jesus said in answer to their questions fell into place like a mosaic does when you see the full picture. Of course, John the Baptist had been a kind of Elijah, it was so obvious, why hadn't we seen it before? But then I realised, nothing, nothing at all would ever be as it was before.......

THE MAN WITH THE SHINING FACE

I love my son. Of course, I love my son, but life hasn't been easy with him. He was very young when we realised that there was something different about him. Other toddlers made noises, they gabbled, they laughed, they interacted with their parents and the world around them. My wife made all kinds of excuses, 'He's just quiet.' 'Not all toddlers are the same.' 'He will grow out of this, you'll see.'

But as he grew, so the convulsions began and then grew worse. He would be thrown to the ground, shaking violently and foaming at the mouth. The realisation began to dawn on us both that our precious son was being tormented by an evil spirit. At this point my wife gave into the grief and each time it overtook him, she would weep and wail for the son she so wanted, but didn't have, and she was filled with grief and love for the son we had, but couldn't help.

Our neighbour, also a dear friend, was the first among many who spoke to us of Jesus and how they had heard He had power to cast out evil, unholy spirits. We'd heard ourselves about the man from the Gerasenes who Jesus had delivered from his torment and was now just like any other man, except he always told everyone about who he used to be and how he came to be as he was.

We talked about it, my wife and I, and we decided there was nothing we could lose by taking him to Jesus. Things couldn't get any worse than they were, or so we thought!

When we found where His disciples were, we fought our way to the front. We could see people leaving who had been made well by the power invested in His disciples. Our faith rose as we asked them to deliver our son from his torment. We had hope and faith that our nightmare would soon be over.

One by one his disciples prayed over our son, but nothing happened. It seemed there was a steady stream of these disciples coming over to us, away from all the other people clamouring for their attention, but one by one they failed miserably to make any difference to our son. My wife began to weep and wail, my faith plummeted with every failed prayer to free our son from the hold of this tormenting spirit.

I had picked him up and we were leaving to go home, all hopes dashed when four more men arrived, well, three ordinary men and Jesus. It was obvious which one Jesus was. He shone, honestly, I know that might sound a daft thing to say, but He did. You know when sunlight lands on a leaf and lights it up almost shining through it and the leaf is transformed? That was how this Jesus looked. My faith which had all but died began again to stir at the sight of this shining man!

He didn't look straight at me but asked His disciples what they'd been doing and talking about. Well at this point I had to speak up. This might be my one and only chance, so I told this man who shone what had happened. I told Him that my son was dumb because of this spirit within him, I told Him how it threw him down, how it made him foam at the mouth, grind his teeth, convulsed him before giving him any respite where he was still. I told Him how my son was wasting away and how I'd brought him to Jesus' disciples to drive out this spirit and how they couldn't do it.

He started talking about lack of faith, of lack of belief, but then told me to bring my son to Him. As we did so and my son saw Jesus, that dreadful spirit overtook him again, threw him to the ground and I looked on in desperation as I had so many, many times before. Jesus asked me how long this had been happening and I told Him, since he was a little boy. I told Him about how this spirit threw him into fire and into water and how it was like this spirit was trying to kill our son. Somehow this man with the shining face brought out of you things you didn't normally tell people, I don't know why, but it seemed right to tell Him.

I ended by saying to Him with all the faith I had left, 'If you can do anything, please have pity on us and help us.' He smiled at that point, which I remember thinking seemed incongruous, but He said, 'Anything at all is possible for him who believes.'
You know I said that He brought out of you things you wouldn't normally say? Well before I'd even thought about what He was saying, I found myself almost weeping as I cried out that I did believe, I do believe, but I needed help with the doubts I had. It wasn't simply a statement of fact, but a cry from my very gut of anguish. I didn't want to not believe enough for my son!
He looked away from me to my son but spoke directly to the spirit within him. He commanded it to come out of him, leave him alone and not go near to him again. There was such authority in that command.
The world sort of stopped at that point as the most horrendous guttural cry came from my son, he convulsed again, but was then still. People around us thought he was dead, but then they hadn't seen this as we had so many, many times before. This time though, Jesus was there, and He went over and took him by the hand, lifting him to his feet and as the colour returned to my son's face, there was something new there, something of the same kind of shining that was in Jesus' face. I remember noticing that before he spoke!
My son spoke! You have no idea how beautiful the sound of your son speaking is when you haven't heard it before. Once I'd grasped that my son was free, my son was well, MY SON COULD TALK, I turned, but Jesus had disappeared with His disciples.

All my hope now was and is still that He knew just how grateful we were, are and always will be and how our whole lives were changed by meeting this man with the shining face, this Jesus!

THE DELAY THAT TOOK US BEYOND DEATH

We counted Him as a friend. Jesus, that is. When He was in Jerusalem, He would stay with us in Bethany. We are, to many, a strange household, my brother Lazarus, my sister Mary, and I, but I really think Jesus saw us as, well as part of His family, but certainly as dear friends. We'd often had Him share meals with us, He knew me well enough you know to rebuke me as one does a sister when I got things wrong. You see I'm the practical one of the three of us. Lazarus is a man and looks after and cares for us, Mary, my sister often has her head in the clouds, living very much at the mercy of her thoughts and feelings, but I'm the practical one. Jesus though, had seen through my facade of busy-ness and had shown me that I shouldn't always seek refuge in what I do but allow myself space to breathe and contemplate and enjoy what is important in life.
Anyway, I digress, for I wanted to tell you about the time when I was confronted with the truth of who Jesus is, who He really is! Not just a 'friend' or a Teacher, but so much more than that.

You see, it began really when Lazarus fell ill. To begin with we did all the things you do when someone falls ill, I made broth, we prayed and watched over him, we called our friends, but there was no improvement and he got worse.

We kept watching over him as the fever took hold of him, sometimes it took both of us to hold him still as he seemed to thrash about in his agony. It was at this point we decided, Mary and I, to send for Jesus. We managed to get someone who knew where He could be found and sent word for Him to come quickly. We told Him that Lazarus, His beloved friend, was very ill.

Whilst we waited for Him to come, we watched and nursed Lazarus, but he got worse and worse. The thrashing stopped, but the fever didn't get any better. He grew paler and paler, became still and then, almost before we realised how bad things were, he died!
We were stunned. We grieved, we wailed. Mary and I prepared him for burial, we both wanted to do that for him, and we buried him in the tomb in our garden.

The house was full of those who had come to support us and mourn with us, yet I think for both of us, the aching void we felt wasn't simply in the loss of our dear brother, but because Jesus wasn't there. We didn't know why, but we did know that He hadn't come.
It was a few days later when someone came running in to me to say that Jesus was coming. I thought I'd better go and warn Him what to expect when He arrived. Did He know that Lazarus had died, or was He still expecting to see him ill, but alive?

When I reached Him, I realised that He knew Lazarus was dead. Of course He knew!
I remember wondering why I ever thought He wouldn't know!

I couldn't help myself, but the words of reproach left my mouth before I remember even thinking them – 'If You'd been here, my brother wouldn't have died, but even now Jesus, I know that whatever You ask Your Father for, He will give to You.'
I'm not sure what I expected Him to do or to say. I know that as the truth of my words sank into my heart, I realised that I really did believe them. I did believe that whatever Jesus asked His Father to do, it would be done and that whatever He did would be good.

I wasn't surprised at His reaction of faith in God, His Father. He reminded me that Lazarus would rise again, and I replied that I knew he would rise again on the last day. His next words jolted me out of such platitudes though!

He said 'I AM myself the Resurrection and the Life. Whoever believes and trusts in Me even if he dies, he shall live. He who continues against all external circumstances to believe in Me shall not die. Martha, do you believe this?'
If you haven't known Jesus as we did, you won't know that tingle that you get down your spine when He says certain things, things that are so deep, so wide, so utterly mind-blowing, yet at the same time so familiar that somehow you've known them to be true all your life, except no-one until this moment has ever been able to paint the picture of them for you. Well, I had one of those moments as He said those words. I knew, I knew what I'd always known, but now, I really KNEW IT!

Almost as if the words themselves were new to me I replied with a sense of wonder, 'I believe that You are the Christ, the Anointed Son of God, the Promised One, the Messiah!' He simply smiled at me in that way He could when you know that He knows what it was you were going to say and was so pleased you'd said it.
I left Him and went to get Mary, still with that sense of wonder within me. Mary was weeping with her friends but went straight away to find Jesus. She told me much later that she had actually said the same thing I had to Him when she found Him! Maybe we're not so different after all, my sister and I!
Anyway, Jesus came and asked where they had laid him and we all went to the tomb. Some of our friends were muttering about Jesus having left it too late to come, but no-one doubted His love for our brother because as we got to the tomb, He wept. He simply wept for His friend, our brother. Even those who had been muttering couldn't deny this outpouring of love and grief from Jesus.

As He gathered Himself, He then said the most extraordinary thing, He told the men to take away the boulder! Lazarus had been in the tomb four days by now, it had been hot so the stench would have been horrific. What was Jesus thinking? I had to say it, but even whilst protesting, I knew there was something He was going to say or do!

What He said was directed at me – 'Didn't I tell you that if you believed in Me, you would see the glory of God?'

'I do believe in You my Lord' was my heart's reply, yet even then, I found myself assenting to His command to remove the stone.
I will be honest, there was no-one there who could have predicted what He would do next, well, even for Jesus this was something else! We'd heard of Him bringing back from the dead Jairus' daughter, but she'd only just died. We'd heard too of the widow in Nain, just about to bury her son, he was on his funeral pyre when Jesus raised him from death, but our dear brother had been in the tomb for four days, his spirit would have departed and his body would have begun to decay, yet Jesus said in a loud voice 'Father, thank You that You hear Me, that You always hear Me. I say this for the benefit of those You have brought here to this place at this time, that they might believe.' He paused, then said in that commanding way only He could, 'Lazarus, come out!'

Walking towards us came our brother, still in his burial cloths! Well, I say walking, but creeping might be better, for we'd bound him beautifully. He still had His burial cloth on his face, Jesus laughed at our reaction and told us through His joyous laughter to help Lazarus free of the binding cloths of death and let him go.
That was all we needed to free us from the daze we were in, which seemed to have frozen us to the spot. We ran to him, to Lazarus, overjoyed at seeing him again, at having had him restored to us.
I knew Jesus was going to do something special. I thought He'd come, and He'd heal him, we'd seen Him do that so many times before, but this......well even for Jesus, this was incredible. He'd told me I would see the glory of God. He'd told me Lazarus would be raised, but this....this, was humbling. I glanced over at Jesus and He met my gaze and smiled. Sometimes you know, words simply get in the way. I could not have expressed anything in words that would have said any more than the look that passed

between us at that point. Just as I had known, He knew. He knew how I felt, how grateful, how full of wonder, how my life would never be what it was before, how I had myself somehow passed from death to life, just as Lazarus had.
He didn't stay with us that time, because our house became such a crowded place where folk who heard about Lazarus would come, just to see him, to see if it was real, to join in our joy. The party and celebration lasted many days and even weeks later after most had gone home, we would still get the occasional knock on the door asking for Lazarus, asking to simply shake his hand, for they wanted to share in the wonder of our resurrected brother.

Even some of the Jewish leaders came, although they weren't full of wonder at all, but filled with scathing scepticism. We showed them the burial cloths and the grave, but they went away as unbelieveing as they arrived.
We, all three of us felt for Jesus, we wished He could have been with us. We understood why He couldn't at that time, but we knew He'd come back again and maybe by then we might have found some words to express our delight and gratitude.........or maybe the wonder was just too great for words!
We talked about it, the three of us, in the stillness when evening draws in. How could we thank Jesus, how could we show Him just what we felt in our gratitude?

We had one thing, our family insurance if you like, our parents had left it to us. It was a pound of pure nard, yes, a pound! In talking it through we all decided that we should give it to Jesus, as an offering of thanks from the three of us.

It was Mary who came up with the idea of anointing Jesus with it, of pouring it out upon Him. We knew the Jewish leaders were planning to kill Him, they'd made it plain enough to Him, but also to us when they came to see Lazarus. They even hinted that it might be better for us if Lazarus was to disappear permanently too!

We knew they meant it, they didn't make idle threats and we knew too that time may be short, so Mary said the next time Jesus came to our home, she'd like to anoint Him with the nard and that we should both be there too, Lazarus and I.

So, about a week before Passover, Jesus came to stay again, on His way to Jerusalem. It was such a joy to the three of us having Jesus there, with Lazarus reclining with Him. I served and Mary prepared herself. At the right point in the meal, we all caught each other's attention and we knew the time was right. It was as though the whole world stood still for a time as Mary uncorked the nard and poured it on Jesus. I found myself crying with Mary as she did so. When I looked at Lazarus, he too was fighting back tears!

I can't describe how beautiful it was, how the fragrance of it filled the room, how there was something deeply spiritual, deeply profound about it. To be honest, we hadn't bargained for the sense of God amongst us that it brought. I know that it wasn't just me that felt it, you could see from other people they too were deeply moved, none more so than Jesus.

After that moment, when the world began to move again, I heard Judas bemoaning the waste of the nard. I didn't like Judas and I suspected his motives for complaining weren't just that it might have been sold for the poor, but that 'poor' Judas might have had some of the proceeds! Well, it hadn't been his to sell anyway, it was our inheritance, ours to do with as we wanted and we had chosen to spend it on Jesus, in grateful thanks for all His amazing goodness to us.

Jesus knew. He knew why, He knew what it cost, He knew it was our sacrifice of thanksgiving to God. He didn't agree with Judas, He said that wherever the story of today was told, the story of this sacrifice would be told too.

We didn't know then what we know now. We didn't have any idea just what significance there was in what Mary had done on our behalf. We didn't realise how short time was for Him, how imminent His death was. I know, maybe we should have, but we didn't.

Now we do know, we are even more humbled to have been a small part of His story, anointing Him for His burial in that way. What was most precious to us, poured out on Him who is most precious to us!

YOU SIMPLY HAD TO BE THERE!

It began like any other day, the busyness of life, the jobs that needed doing and the conversations I need to have. My business thrived on all three of those things and that day, I needed to have a conversation and do a bit of business with Matthias.

I made my way to his place but got caught by a couple of other men I do business with sometimes who wanted to talk with me. I was happily listening to them, having been told Matthias was over the other side of town concluding some deals of his own.

As we talked a group of men came up to Matthias' place, took hold of his donkey, an unridden colt, quite a rarity. It was tied to the gate and they went to make off with it. These men were Galileans, so we were watching out for them, no doubt all of us thinking of the folklore saying, 'Nothing good ever came out of Galilee!' Obviously, we weren't going to simply let them walk off with his donkey. He may not actually have been there, but we were his colleagues and yes, his friends, and we certainly weren't going to allow that to happen.

We challenged them, asking them indignantly 'Who do you think you are? What do you think you're doing? That's Matthias' donkey, where do you think you're taking it?' Their reply floored us somewhat, 'The Lord, the Master has need of it and will return it once the need is fulfilled.'

We let them go, simply because as we looked at them someone thought they were the friends of a teacher called Jesus and we knew that Matthias had listened to this Galilean rabbi, Jesus. He'd told us that at one point he'd been travelling around, on business and had stopped, just for a breather, to listen to Jesus. He ended up staying for the rest of the day, along with thousands of others. He was just getting ready to go home as it was getting late, but this Jesus said to his disciples that they should feed the crowd! Ridiculous, I know, but according to Matthias, this rabbi's disciples did just that and Matthias reckoned it was the best bread and fish supper he'd ever had!

So, we knew that it was perfectly possible that he had given permission, but, it's hard to explain really, we all said afterwards, there was no way we could have said no! Not that we didn't think we could, or that we didn't care enough to, but just that, well, just that there was something more going on behind it all. This Galilean rabbi had caused some upset, especially with the teachers of the law, and had definitely rubbed them up the wrong way, calling them whitewashed tombs! Some of us were impressed not only at the audacity, but actually knew that He had hit the nail on the head with that – as businessmen, we sometimes saw the other side of those 'upright' Pharisees and the Sadducees too.

I think it was what began to happen after we'd allowed them to take the colt..... We sauntered after them, partly to check where they were doing – you can't always trust Galileans, but also partly because we were intrigued! Now, I crave your indulgence here, I know this is going to sound, well, weird, but like I say, you simply had to have been there.

As we walked some way behind them, we saw Jesus join them and sit on the colt – interesting because I know donkeys who have never been ridden before – they can be tricky blighters! But no, Jesus just got on this colt, and it walked away as though it had been used to carrying loads all its life! Then, folk began to throw down their cloaks, tear branches off the palm trees and began to say 'Hosanna'. It got louder and we all, without exception, got caught up in the growing crowd and the swelling cries 'Blessed is He who comes in the name of the Lord.' 'Messiah, save now' 'Hosanna'.

As we entered Jerusalem proper, through the gates, the shouts and cries became deafening. It seemed like the whole of Jerusalem was acknowledging this Galilean rabbi as the Messiah, me included! You might call it 'mass hysteria', you might refer to it as mass hypnosis or something more sinister, but, like I said, you had to have been there, it was like nothing I'd ever encountered before. It was as if the world became clearer somehow, as if the truth was so glaringly obvious, you wondered how you could not have seen it earlier. Jesus is the Messiah, the King of the Jews, the Son of David! Even now as I say those words, the truth hits me again between the eyes!

As we travelled through the streets of Jerusalem, the Pharisees and teachers of the law were getting really very angry and seriously ticked off. They told Jesus to stop people from saying these things, but He replied, and I completely believed Him, 'If these people didn't shout out this as truth, the very stones themselves would do it for them!' He was right! It was as if anything, anything at all was possible in that moment, even stones crying out, a never before ridden colt meekly carrying this Messiah amid all the noise and clamour, the whole of Jerusalem shouting as with one voice the fulfilment of their longing for this Messiah and their acknowledgment that He was here.

I never did my business with Matthias, I left that place changed. I understood why Matthias had been changed, I could believe that fish and bread supper was the best meal ever. I wasn't sure what the next few days and weeks would hold, but I reckoned it would change the world and I wanted to be a part of it!

HEARING THE IMPOSSIBLE

It was just another shift, another arrest, another duty in Jerusalem. My name is Malchus and I'm a slave of the high priest in Jerusalem! We were on a high state of alert because it was the Jewish Passover and there had been rumours of a rebellion or an uprising ever since some guy had ridden through the gates about a week ago on a donkey. Didn't make any sense to me anyway because if you were going to lead some kind of rebellion, or mastermind some kind of coup, why would you come riding in on a donkey for goodness' sake? You'd choose a big black stallion or something, anything, but not a flaming donkey!

Anyway, this particular evening we were called out to arrest some Galilean on the Mount of Olives. It's a lovely place that garden over there. Gethsemane, they call it. Apparently in their Hebrew it means olive press! There are certainly enough olives there, but it is very pretty, peaceful like. This was a night watch though, so we couldn't see much. We were being led by some Jew who had been a friend of the guy we were going to arrest, but had turned Him in. That doesn't sit well with me or with any of us you know, don't like it when someone turns against a mate. We'd all felt the same, it felt a bit dodgy being led by this bloke. It seemed like he'd set some kind of trap and we were the ones who were about to spring the damn thing. Not good, but still, that's our job and we have to do it.

Off we went with the flaming torches. I couldn't make out why there were so many of us just for one man, but mine wasn't to question why! We got to the garden and the bloke leading us walked right past three men asleep on the ground. Vagrants I guessed. He goes up to this bloke who had been kneeling, praying it looked like, as we'd walked up to Him. This Judas – the bloke leading us, went up and kissed Him, and the other bloke, Jesus, asked him if he'd come to betray Him with a kiss. That was like a double whammy, and I could see this Jesus was upset. Made me mad really, it's just not the way to do things.

It was at that point the three who I'd thought were vagrants jumped up to this Jesus' defence. One bloke, big burly fisherman he was, had a sword. He had no flaming idea how to use the damn thing but use it he did and caught my ear. It was a bloody mess and I saw my ear sliced right off, on the ground.

Everything went black at that point – blood everywhere, shouting all over the place and everything sounding strange – well I guess it would, my bloody ear was on the ground in that beautiful place! Next thing I knew, in amongst all the blackness and horror and strangeness of sound I hear one voice! I know that sounds a bit weird as there were probably lots of voices, but having fallen to my knees with the pain, all I heard was this one voice telling the fisherman that this wasn't the way and I felt the voice touch my ear, well, where my ear had been.

It didn't hurt when He touched it. Well, actually, no, it did, but it was a very strange sensation, the pain from the swords cut stopped being unbearable and became gloriously excruciating!
Look, I don't expect you to understand, but just take my word for it, it did. Next thing I know the pain has gone; everything sounds normal again, and my ear is fine. I mean, fully fine. I mean, my ear that was on the ground was still there, but I had a new ear and there was no pain. I HAD A NEW EAR! I looked at this Jesus as the rest of our troop had hold of Him and there was a look. He didn't say anything, but there was just that look. My hand went to feel my ear, my new ear and as I looked again at this Jesus it was as though He smiled. I know He can't have because my mates were manhandling Him at that point putting the shackles on Him to lead Him away, but that's what I remember.

Well, we arrested Him, we took Him to the courthouse, but the whole thing went by me in a blur. I was trying to make it all make sense! Why did this itinerant preacher from Galilee heal my ear? He had just been dobbed in by his mate, was being arrested, one of his other mates had tried to fight for him and I'd copped the fallout, nothing unusual there, but....in all that, why did this guy Jesus forget everything else and heal my ear? No, not just heal it, regrow it, make it better than it was before? Why would you do that?

But He did.

FAILURE!

I'm Peter. I'm a fisherman and quite honestly right now, I reckon I'm a complete failure!

I realise you have no idea what I'm talking about, so I need to go back to about three years ago, when it started. I was with Andrew, my brother, tending to our nets after a night's fishing. A man came by and called to us both to come follow Him and He would make us fishers of men! Now, let's be honest, it's not normally the kind of thing we would do, Andrew and I, but somehow this guy was different! I can't explain it any other way, so off we went.

We left our nets and followed Him. I know that sounds irresponsible, even vaguely ridiculous, but if it does, you definitely don't know Jesus. When He calls, you follow, when He speaks there is authority and wherever He walks miracles happen, but also confusion and opposition follow!

Anyway, I'm getting off the point. It's been a wild ride these last three years. I've seen and experienced stuff that is completely beyond normal life. My mother-in-law was miraculously healed, as were countless others. Lepers, paralytics, blind men, demon possessed, even dead children brought back to life. I've seen them all. I've been there as He fed thousands with a few loaves and a couple of fish, I've watched as He has simply spoken and storms have died instantly, I've even walked on water, though I stuffed that up too!

I've just come from the courtyard of the High Priest, it's the middle of the night and Jesus, my friend, rabbi, and the Messiah has been arrested, falsely accused and condemned as a blasphemer and traitor and I've just lied three times, denying I ever knew Him. That's no way to treat a friend and I'm utterly ashamed. I confess to you, so ashamed that I cried, sobbed like a baby!

Thing is, now I think on it, it's not the first time by a long stretch that I've mucked up. There was that time I walked on the water as Jesus was doing, yes, honestly He was, but I sank – man those waves were high! He rescued me that time.

I remember too, being up on a mountain with Jesus, James and John and I can't even begin to put into words what happened up there. Jesus turned into an incredible Light-being, like an angel, but way more – I told you it wouldn't make sense in words! Anyway, I muessed up again then, thinking I could build shelters for us all to stay there. Daft idea, I realise that now, but in the heat of the moment, it seemed to make sense.

Then there was the time we'd been asked a question by Jesus on who we thought He was – so many theories were being spouted at the time, especially as it was just after John had been killed, but I was pretty vocal and absolutely categoric that Jesus was, well, He is, the Messiah. I even managed to muff that up though. He began to talk after that about how the Messiah was going to suffer, how He would be taken away and beaten. I mean, if He is the Messiah, He really shouldn't be talking like that, so I took Him to one side and told Him so.
He turned on me, called me Satan and told me to get behind Him. Well, I'd clearly got that one totally wrong, hadn't I? He'd been so touched and delighted when I'd spoken in faith about who He was and so to straight away, have catastrophically messed up was pretty spectacular, even for me!

Back to this evening. We'd shared a Passover meal together, all 12 of us and Jesus. It was one of those precious times where you feel some kind of weight of significance somehow, not just because it's Passover, but something more than that. Dunno what exactly,

but Jesus spent time talking about the bread being His body and not drinking the wine again until the Kingdom had come. It was a bit different from the usual Passover stuff, but it didn't all make a whole lot of sense, except for that feeling of it being important, significant somehow. He'd been talking a lot about these kind of things recently and quite honestly it was beginning to get a bit unnerving.
After that, Jesus began to talk about one of us betraying Him. I said I'd never do that, no matter what. Well, I wouldn't, would I? We all pretty much felt the same. At some point Judas got up after talking to Jesus and went off. At the time, I didn't read much into that. Judas had been a bit funny of late and often went off, so we thought no more of it. How were we to know, seriously, how could we have seen?

Here I am, only a few hours after all that, (you'll find it hard to believe it is only a few hours. when I tell you what's happened since.) We went off to the Olive Press garden on the hillside – Gethsemane. We'd been there many times before with Jesus. He liked to pray there and apart from being beautiful, it is a pretty special place. This time, He only took me, James and John, which wasn't unusual, He'd done that many times. He asked us simply to watch and pray. Well, it had been a busy day, we'd had a meal and quite honestly, all of us were knackered. Jesus went off by Himself, just a little distance away, to pray.

I tried, honestly, I tried to stay awake, but you know what it's like when you're dog tired and your eyelids simply close without your permission, well that was me, but it was also true for James and John. We were all just so exhausted. Jesus came back a couple of times, each time saying to us all, effectively, 'Couldn't you just watch with me, stay awake, pray for just this time?' I failed Him then and it didn't get any better.

In fact, it was about to get a whole lot worse. A whole gaggle of the Chief priests' henchmen arrived, with Judas! That woke us up I can tell you. That snake went up to Jesus, and we heard Him say

'Would you betray me with a kiss, Judas?' I'd had a vague inkling something was going to kick off, what with all His talk of betrayal and I'd come prepared and brought a sword. Well, I wasn't having them take Jesus without me putting up a fight, was I? Now, I'm no swordsman, but I managed to catch one of the henchmen with it and sliced off his ear. But rather than it encouraging Jesus that I was fighting for Him, showing Him how much He meant to me and how I wasn't going to allow this to happen, Jesus turned on me, 'What do you think you're doing Peter? Don't you think I could call on twelve legions of angels?'
'Well do it then!' I screamed at Him, but He simply turned away and healed the bloke's ear. Well, I say healed it, actually he grew another ear in place of the one on the ground in the dust! It caused quite a stir, amidst the commotion. Not surprising really. I didn't take a lot of notice after that – I'm out of my depth here, I thought!

They took Him away, then. Took Him to the Chief Priest's palace. They were going to conduct some sort of kangaroo court trial, like they did when they couldn't get what they wanted. Trumped up charges are their speciality at times like those. I followed behind, well quite a way behind to be honest, after all, it wouldn't make sense to be seen, would it?
It was cold and I was trying to blend in with those in the courtyard, but then some woman came and said I was one of Jesus' followers. Well, I wouldn't get to hear what was going on and show Jesus I was there for Him if I admitted it and they'd have arrested me too. So, in order to shut her up, I lied and said I didn't know Him.

I walked away and over to the fire, but the woman was one of those who wouldn't let it drop! She followed me and said it again, adding that I must be one of Jesus' followers because I was from Galilee, like He was. I was getting a bit freaked by now, so was pretty vehement in my denial that time.
After a third time of denying I even knew Jesus and getting even more angry about it, the cock crowed. Nothing monumental in

that, but for me it certainly was! The realisation hit me right between the eyes, that this was exactly what Jesus had said I'd do and I'd only gone and done it. I turned to look at where He was – I could see Him through the window and He turned and looked at me.
He knew.
He knew I'd done it, knew I'd denied Him, not once, not twice, but three times.
I looked away and I wept like a baby.

Tell me I'm not a complete failure now! See, you can't, can you?
I don't know what is going to happen in the next few hours, what they'll do to Him, but I know what the law says about blasphemers, so it's not good. Jesus has been saying stuff about suffering and even about dying, but not like this.
Surely it cannot end like this? It can't end with Him knowing I'm a failure and Him dying, it just can't. Can it?

CURSED AND CRUCIFIED

We all stood there, at the foot of those three crosses on Golgotha's hill. The sky was dark, almost as if night had come early to cover up this dreadful injustice. It seemed like forever that we stood there, powerless to do anything other than wait. Despite the horror of the previous few hours where we saw Jesus carry the cross, when we heard His anguished cries as He was nailed, hand and foot to that cursed instrument of torture, when we heard the sickening thud as the cross was lifted upright and sunk into its prepared hole - that thud which will remain with me forever and Jesus' cry as the force of it shook his whole bruised and battered body; when we had heard the priests and the soldiers spit their venom at Him, taunting Him, despite all else they had done, they simply couldn't help themselves being the snakes in the grass they truly are.
Despite all of that, we still hoped, still dared to hope that He would come down from that cross, that He would work another miracle, that He would come down in glory with God's angels. But His breathing got worse, more laboured, more painful. Louder and louder until all I could hear were these rasping, gasping breaths in the darkness. Time had no meaning any more.... We were there with that sound, and it felt like forever.

Jesus looked down at us all and saw His mum, Mary, there. He looked at John and told him to take care of her. How like Jesus that was - thinking of someone else even though He was there on that wretched cross, dying!

It was 3 o'clock, though it felt later, when suddenly Jesus Himself cried out. The sound of His laboured breathing was bad enough, but to hear that cry of abandonment from Him who spoke constantly of His close relationship with His Father, was heart-breaking, gut-wrenching and was the most hopeless cry I had ever heard in my life. 'My God, my God, why have You abandoned me?' If God had abandoned Him, what hope for the rest of us? We all knew then that He wasn't coming down, that there would be no glorious angelic visitation, that there was only one way this was going to end.

Someone tried to give Him some of that bitter wine they keep by the crosses, revolting stuff, and it was then we became aware that the chief priests and others who had insulted Him and spat out their venom at Him were still there, still watching, waiting like we were, but the darkness had hidden them. They couldn't hear Him properly; they were too far away, and they thought He was calling Elijah! It was almost funny, them being so clever and all, not even knowing that what Jesus had really said was worse than that, so very much worse.

It didn't matter anyway, they could say what they liked now, do what they liked now, none of it mattered anyway. Jesus was dying. Jesus had been abandoned by God, His Father. Jesus, our hope, our friend, Jesus the miracle-worker, the freedom-giver, the One who they proclaimed as Messiah less than a week ago as He rode into Jerusalem on that donkey. JESUS WAS DYING.

His breathing was getting louder, but there were gaps between the breaths now, horrible deathly long gaps. Then, He cried out again, but this was a different cry, a cry more like the Jesus we knew, a cry that said, 'IT IS FINISHED.'

Then.....silence.........for a few seconds which seemed like hours.

I remember thinking at the time that He sounded as though He'd beaten something, but then, that silence........

I know it can only have been for a few seconds, because then we heard and felt the earthquake and there were people shouting

about graves being broken open, about dead being raised to life. Why were they surprised? Jesus had died, but that enormous death, like a millstone thrown into still water had to have caused ripples. Someone came running to those priests and told them that the curtain of the temple had been torn in two from top to bottom - imagine that! Top to bottom it had been torn in two. Just at the time Jesus died, that huge curtain tore.
We had no idea what it all meant, but we knew it was all to do with Jesus, even the priests knew that much, but where it brought a glimmer of light in that dreadful darkness to us that Jesus was still who He had said He was, it freaked them out! We were all still left though with the fact that Jesus was dead.

Joseph came then, a guy who had spent time with us and with Jesus. He asked to take Jesus' body and offered a grave, the grave he had planned for his burial. They said he could take Jesus' body, so we all set to bringing His body down and preparing it, Joseph had brought the embalming creams and cloths - I remember being so grateful for that. We hadn't thought of it, we were so absorbed in being there with Jesus, we hadn't given any thought to afterwards!

The men took His wrapped body to the beautiful tomb in a lovely garden and placed Him in the tomb. We closed it and then waited. I have no idea why we waited then, we were simply numb and wanted even then to somehow be near Him, so we waited, we sat, holding each other in a vain attempt at comfort, though none could be found.

After some little while soldiers came to the grave. If I could have felt anything, I would have felt anger then, but I couldn't feel anything. It turned out that the priests had said we might steal Jesus' body and say He had been raised from death as He said He would. How typical of them to think we would be as devious as them. It hadn't occurred to us because the worst had happened.

JESUS WAS DEAD!

IT WAS THE LEAST I COULD DO

Some miscarriages of justice are inevitable, we're only human after all. We might be learned, we might be part of the Jewish council of priests in God's holy city, but there are times, before Elohim Adonai, I admit, we get it wrong.

This was more than simply getting it wrong though. This miscarriage of justice was a vendetta! Jesus had upset so many people, not by preaching evil, nor by harming people, or by breaking the essence of the Torah. In fact, He spent these last few years, throughout our land doing exactly the opposite of that. He healed those who came to Him, from the leper to the lame, from the deaf to the demon possessed, there was no-one He could not help and nothing it seemed that He was incapable of doing, well unless you count upsetting the establishment, that is.

We'd been summoned to a trial at Caiaphas' home. I have often found it difficult to reconcile these effectively illegal court proceedings we are summoned to. They usually take place at night and that adds to my discomfort. Thinking of deeds done in darkness and all that means before God is never far from my mind. However, summoned we were.

I'd heard they were making a concerted effort of going after Jesus, this unassuming teacher from Nazareth. Unassuming, but with the authority of heaven behind Him, as you'd know if you had heard Him. Nicodemus and I really wanted no part of this kangaroo court. We had listened to Jesus, not to pick holes in what He said, nor to trip Him up, or trick Him into saying something that could be used against Him. In fact, there were several times Nicodemus and I caught each other's eyes when time after time,

He outwitted quite clever questions and gave answers that no-one expected.

All that simply inflamed anger in many of the other members of the Sanhedrin. They saw Him as a huge danger to our standing. They felt He undermined our authority and threatened our livelihood, not to mention our standing in the community here in Jerusalem. Most of them had spent much of their wealth to gain their positions, worked hard to get where they were, so weren't going to give that up easily. So, they were delighted when one of His disciples, Judas Iscariot, came to offer to present Him to us. I didn't trust Judas. There was talk of him being sympathetic to the Maccabean rebellion, which was rumbling in the background again, as it had done before in our history.

So, having arrested Him, we had our court proceedings. What a shambles. Rogues drafted in to bring their 'witness' accounts to His crimes, each one a complete fabrication and a mockery of all that is good and decent. To say that Nicodemus and I were uncomfortable doesn't come close to describing how we felt. I was ashamed of my priesthood to be honest. Were we really reduced to this? We hated it, but what could either of us actually do?

Obviously, He was found guilty, having made a comment about the Son of Man being seated at the right hand of God and attributing that to Himself, there was, I know, no way back from that. You can't align yourself with God and not be called a blasphemer! Yet, somehow, I wonder, yet again, if He isn't actually who He says He is!

We were 'encouraged' to witness the crucifixion! Some of my fellow priests debased themselves by hurling insults at Him, bruised and bloodied on the cross. I found that at best distasteful and at worst downright demeaning to their role. It served to show, I guess, just how much He had got under their skin!
I watched. Nicodemus and I stood together. We saw the women, His mother amongst them, wailing. I couldn't, but there was a

part of me that wanted to wail with them.

We saw the way He died. We heard the Roman centurion speak out the words of faith that 'Truly, this was the Son of God!' I agreed with Him and grieved, just as much as the wailing women at the foot of that cross.

It was something He said on the cross that got to me. He'd been hanging there for almost 6 hours when He spoke. I was shocked He even had the strength to do that. He spoke to the only one of His disciples that was there, I think they call him John. He gave him charge of His mother Mary! In all that pain, He was a good Jewish boy, thinking of His mother. Then, He yelled 'Father, forgive them, they don't realise what they're doing!' I had begun to realise what we'd done, but it certainly didn't make me feel any better!
He then said, with a sort of triumph in His tone 'It is completed'! I looked up at Him at that point, and you may think it fanciful, but it was at that point He deliberately gave up His life, He died, intentionally!

Some of the other priests were called away at that point, apparently the curtain in the temple had been torn in two, from top to bottom. Well, the sky was dark, there had been an earthquake, so I wasn't wholly surprised at implications from the earthquake. I admit though, it was strange if it had torn from top to bottom!

I didn't go. I stayed. I wanted to be there, even though He had died. There began forming in my mind, in my heart, growing and growing, a determination to do something, to stand up for this man who was the Messiah. I was sure of it now, but I was too late, wasn't I? What could I do?

My mind thought of my grave. I'd had it for a while, chosen by me, for its beautiful setting, in a garden. The idea grew, despite the implications for me, for my family, for my standing in the community, for my very membership of the Sanhedrin. It grew and grew, like a plant, like a flower within. I may not have stood up for Him in His life, but I could provide a fitting grave for the King of the Jews. Salome would understand, eventually. My children would forgive me, I was sure, but I had to do this.

Nicodemus and I went to Pilate. We asked for His body, knowing he would have to check Jesus was dead, especially with the rumours about Him having said He would rise from the dead. Pilate gave his permission having checked with his officials. But even then, I realised that behind me were other members of the Sanhedrin, calling for an armed guard to be placed at the tomb, so His disciples didn't steal the body, claiming He had risen! It's amazing how their thoughts of other people's actions simply revealed the depth of their own twisted and warped thinking! That too was granted by Pilate, so Nicodemus and I went off to take down Jesus' body. I collected some linen to wrap Him in along the way.

The women were still there and were very frightened when Nicodemus and I arrived but wept anew with relief when they realised what we had planned to do. His mother fell at my feet, crying with gratitude. I gently told her to get up and help us, that it was the very least I could do for Him, not having been able to prevent His death.
The women all helped us, and I was touched to the core to see my wife, Salome, amongst them. We placed Him in the tomb and the stone was rolled over the entrance. It took 4 of us to do it, but we managed it, and He had been given a burial place of beauty, despite His 'cursed' death on a cross.

It may not have been much, it may be just a sop in the grand scheme of things, but it was all I could do and the least He deserved.

THE RESURRECTION

We were in the Upper room. It had become where we spent most of our time now..... The new now, after what happened on Friday.

Somehow being together made what we had learned and what we had thought and seen and given our lives to for three years more, well more as though it hadn't been a complete waste of time. We were still raw with all that had happened just three days ago, on Friday.
Was it only three days? Those three days might just as well have been three years for it seemed to us then that we couldn't really remember things Jesus had said when He was with us, because you see, Jesus was dead and that changed everything!
All we had given up, all the hope we had placed in Him, gone. We couldn't go back to our lives before because to do so seemed like ultimately admitting that we had wasted three years on this man who we thought was the Messiah, who we had thought would save His people, just as David and the prophets had said the Messiah would, but He, Jesus, was dead.

I couldn't believe it was a waste, I couldn't believe it had all been in vain, yet......here we were. We all seemed to lurch one after another from despair, to grief, to acceptance and round, again and again like a never-ending circle.

So, it's Sunday.
It's morning and as we stir from the dreamless sleep of the exhausted, we realised that Mary Magdalene and the other Mary had gone. They said they would, they wanted to take the spices to anoint His body. None of the rest of us could face it really, brought

it home too much, I guess.
Before we'd had time to collect our thoughts even, the two of them arrived back. They were really upset - 'They've taken Him, they've taken Him...He's not there.'
At that point it was Peter and I that looked at one another and without a word, ran. We didn't need to ask who or where, we simply ran as though our lives depended on it, for in every way that is important, our lives did depend on it. We ran to the tomb.
Sure enough, the guards were gone - they'd gone back to the priests we assumed, but what of the body? What was the point of them taking His body? The stone wasn't across the face of the tomb - the stone wasn't even in its groove; it was clean out and leaning against the side of the tomb - I remember thinking how strange that was. All these things run through your mind in milliseconds as you run towards your goal. I got there first, Peter couldn't keep up, but I stood there trying to make sense of it.
When Peter caught up with me, he went straight into the tomb itself. I followed and saw there was nothing there. Well, I say nothing, but there was, there were the burial cloths. I'd seen Joseph wrap His poor broken lifeless body in them on that awful Friday, just three days previously, but here they were folded in this tomb. Even the one we wrapped around His bloodied head was rolled up at the end.

It was at that point like my mind suddenly became freed to remember what He'd said. You see, He'd said this, He'd said He would rise, He'd known He would die and He said He'd rise. Was it actually all true? Had He risen, risen from death?
Belief and hope flooded my whole body. If He had, if it was true, then everything fell back into place like the picture you see when a mosaic is complete. We'd seen fragments before, but now, I thought, for the first time, I think I am beginning to see something of that full picture. I needed thinking time, so I went home to ponder.
Mary told us she wanted to wait behind at the tomb, she said she felt closer to Him there, even though His body had gone. I'm so

glad she did because of what happened next.

I hadn't been home too long when Mary arrived at my door, I'd left her weeping by that tomb, but this was a very different Mary, banging on our door and babbling....'Angels....seen Him....risen....like-He-said'

We all met back then in the Upper room. What a difference from the mood of the morning! We almost didn't dare believe it, but when we all listened together to what Mary had seen - angels telling her He had risen, then turning and seeing Him and Him speaking her name and knowing it was Him just confirmed what Peter and I had almost not dared to believe, despite with all our hearts wanting to believe that all He had said was true. That He is the Son of Man and He has risen from being dead!
But before we could fully digest what had happened to Mary, and what she was telling us, He was there! Honestly, He was suddenly just, there! He looked at us all and said, 'Peace to you!'

My first thought was that it really was only 4 days ago when He'd last said that to us in this very room, where He'd explained that His peace wasn't like the peace the world gives. So very much had happened since then, but now, here He was, risen from the dead.
As I looked at Him there was something of that brilliance and radiance Peter, James and I had seen when we went up and saw Him transfigured before us, yet it was Jesus. It was the Jesus we'd all known for so long.

Jesus was alive!

Jesus had risen! How can I describe how it felt to you? It was like having lived all your life in a cave and coming out suddenly into sunlight with all its warmth, colour, light and beauty.
When He held out His hands and spoke peace to us, we could see the nail marks on His hands. I looked at His feet and there the nail marks were. I remember thinking there was no doubting it really was Jesus.

I wanted to laugh, to cry, to jump, to hug Him, to dance and to ask Him a million questions, but there was time for that. For now, it was enough that He was here.

Jesus IS alive!

Printed in Great Britain
by Amazon